The MAGIC

Healing Rock

To

May God Bless
you abundantly

Elva

Written by Elva Beers Hainzey

Illustrated by Brianna Masters

ISBN 978-1-63630-805-0 (Paperback)
ISBN 978-1-63630-806-7 (Digital)

Covenant Books, Inc.
11661 Hwy 707
Murrells Inlet, SC 29576
www.covenantbooks.com

This book is dedicated to Morgan Christopher Hainzey, my son, whom God chose to take to heaven at the age of fifteen. I'm looking forward to strolling over heaven with him as he shows me what all God has prepared for us.

I want to thank Jesus, my Lord and Savior who gave me the idea and words of this book. Most of all for the forgiveness of my sins.

I want to thank my husband Chuck for providing the finances to publish this book.

I want to thank my daughters Dorothea and Vandana for all their help.

I want to thank Brianna Masters for the beautiful illustrations for this book.

I want to thank Suzy Carr, Renee Barnhill and everyone at Covenant Books Publishing for all of their help.

Bug Box

A young boy named Morgan loved God's creation. From the time he could walk, his favorite thing to do was to go exploring God's creation, especially the bugs, insects, and animals.

One of his favorite places on earth was Light and Life Christian Campground in Mansfield, Ohio. He and his mom would go to the Kids Camp there in the summer, his mom to work at the camp and Morgan to go exploring. Oh, the things that he would find. Morgan's dad made him a bug box so he could put his findings in to look at for a while and then let them go.

One day during camp, Morgan found a cicada still in its shell.

Even the workers were excited about it and told Morgan, "If it starts breaking out of its shell, let us know, we want to watch it."

A few days later, the cicada started to come out of its shell, and the adult workers were crowding around Morgan to watch it. How awesome it was to watch it come out of its shell just like a butterfly.

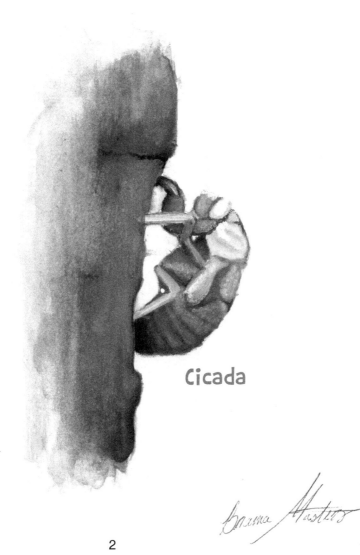

Cicada

Another time when the camp was going to the lake to swim, the bus broke down between two cornfields. Everyone was upset—that is, except for Morgan. While they waited for another bus to pick them up, Morgan asked his mom if he could go exploring in the cornfield. The stalks were four or five feet tall.

She said, "Just along the edge."

Wouldn't you know it, Morgan found a praying mantis. Morgan sure became popular. All the kids wanted to see it.

Praying mantis

3

Great horned owl

Then they saw the yellow camp bus coming to take them to the lake. Morgan's mom told him to leave the praying mantis in the cornfield. Of course, Morgan was upset; it was his prized possession. He reluctantly let it go, got on the bus, and they headed to the lake.

One night at camp after Morgan's mom got him settled in bed in their dorm, she went outside to go to the restrooms when she heard some commotion and saw Dale, the caretaker of the campground, with some other workers. Dale had a big spotlight shining up in one of the large trees on the campground. She went over to see what was going on, and Dale had the light on a great horned owl.

Skull

He said, "As long as the light is on it, it won't fly away."

So she told him to keep the light on it, she was going to get Morgan. When Morgan saw it, he couldn't believe how big it was. As soon as Dale took the light off the owl, you could hear the fluttering of wings as it flew away. You never knew what Morgan had in his pockets or bug box at camp. Usually toads, caterpillars, butterflies. He loved all that God created.

Another favorite place of God's creation for Morgan was Revere, Pennsylvania, where his grandmother lived. Morgan called her GG because she was his cousin's great-grandma, and they called her GG. So he did too. GG had emphysema. She smoked for many years, and it damaged her lungs. That's why you should never smoke. The body is the temple of God. 1 Corinthians 6:19 NKJV says, "Or do you not know that your body is the temple of the Holy Spirit who is in you, whom you have from God and you are not your own?" GG quit smoking, but not before it damaged her lungs.

Every summer, they went to his grandma's for two weeks. Revere, Pennsylvania, was a small community of about five hundred people. It was safe for Morgan to go out exploring the beautiful creation that God made. One day, Morgan was out exploring, and in the green meadows where the cattle roamed, he found a cow's skull.

Three-tier wasp nest

Wow! He couldn't wait to get back to GG's to show them what he found. Another day, he found a three tier wasp nest over by his great-uncle's chicken farm.

He thought, *How lucky I am!* He couldn't wait to show it to his science teacher. It just seemed like God always helped him to find these unique things. Another time he was exploring down where the rows of coke ovens were,

Coke ovens

Deer drinking water

As a deer Pantenth for the water so my soul longeth after thee.
You alone are my heart's desire and I long to Worship thee.

he found a partial deer leg with the hoof. It made him feel sad that someone would do that to such a beautiful creature. He thought of the scripture in Psalm 42:1 NKJV: *"As the deer pants for the water brooks, so pants my soul for You, O God."* His favorite song was "As a Deer Panteth."

Morgan knew he had to be back at GG's before dark. He would be so dirty from exploring all day.

Morgan dirty

Johnny-jump-ups

One night, he was trying to get something out of his socks when he was getting ready for a bath.

His mother said, "Here, let me help. What do you have in there anyways?"

Morgan said, "Fishing worms."

His mother said, "Ooh," and pulled her hand back and said, "you get them."

You never knew what you were going to find in Morgan's pant pockets or socks. When he was done bathing, it wasn't a black bathtub ring he left; you were lucky to find any white on the tub! Off to bed he went, said his prayers, and kissed his mom good night. Then dreaming of what he was going to explore the next day.

The next morning after breakfast, Morgan was off to explore again. Today he thought he would explore the woods right up the hill from GG's. It was a beautiful, sunshiny day with blue skies filled with puffy cumulus clouds. He thought of Psalm 118:24 NKJV, which says, *"This is the day the Lord has made, we will rejoice and be glad in it."* This was the woods where his mother used to play as a child, swinging on the cable swing that would swing way out over the ravine, swinging on a grapevine that, when she and her friend decided to ride it together, broke with them on it.

Fortunately, no one got hurt. She would love to eat black cherries off the tree, pick Johnny-jump-ups with her cousin, and sometimes she would go running out of the woods from a garter snake. Morgan loved snakes. Hoped he would find some today. He remembered one time at Light and Life Christian Campground, he found a PVC pipe with about a dozen baby snakes in it. His mom would always tell him to leave animals or insects in their natural habitat. He had no problem then because they were living in a PVC pipe, but his mom made him leave them on the campground anyway. When Morgan got to the woods, he was surprised to see the paths were all grown over. He thought, *What the kids are missing out on by being on their electronics.* He also thought, with the paths overgrown, he just might find some snakes.

As he walked along, he would look under rocks. He always looked under rocks because you never know what interesting thing you might find under them, like snakes, sow bugs, salamanders, or fishing worms, just to name a few.

Snake

Chicken Hawk

As he walked along, he saw an orange monarch butterfly gliding through the air; he saw a chicken hawk up in a tree, a chipmunk with stripes down his back, and when he ran, his tail would stick straight up. He saw a bunny over by a log nibbling on grass. Then he saw a dragonfly fly overhead. He thought, *I almost caught one of those unique insects.* The trees of the woods kept the hot sun off him.

As he walked along, he saw some mysterious light in a distance. He thought, *What's that?* As he got closer, he saw it was a rock by a tree that had a light coming out from under it. There was a sign by it that said, "Magic Healing Rock."

That made Morgan think about the scripture Psalm 62:6 NKJV: "*He only is my Rock and my salvation.*" The rock was not magic. Magic is an illusion, but God's power is real. It was the power of God within it. Scripture says in Luke 19:39–40 NKJV, "And some of the Pharisees called to him from the crowd, 'Teacher, rebuke Your disciples.' But He answered and said to them, 'I tell you that if they should keep silent, the stones would immediately cry out.'" In other words, if the people won't worship God, the rocks will cry out in worship.

The key to healing is to worship the sovereign God. Morgan thought of GG with the emphysema and said, "I'm going to take this rock back to GG." It was about the size of a loaf of pumpernickel bread. Maybe the Magic Healing Rock (Jesus) would heal her. He knew the light coming out from under the rock was God's power. As he was coming down the road leading to GG's, his mother spotted him coming and saw this light coming from something he was carrying. She thought, *What does he have now!*

As he got closer, she said, "Morgan, what do you have?"

He said, "I found this rock in the woods. It had a sign by it that said, 'Magic Healing Rock.'"

His mom said, "We don't believe in magic, it is an illusion."

Morgan said, "Well, the Bible says Jesus is our Rock, and He is our Healer, so maybe the Magic Healing Rock means that our Rock, Jesus, has the power to heal. I think the light coming from this rock is Jesus's healing power. I'm hoping it will heal GG, but it wasn't God's will to heal GG here on earth. The Healing Rock (Jesus) gave GG the ultimate healing when He took her home to heaven with Him."

Morgan missed GG, but knew she could now breathe without oxygen and walk again. Seven years later, when Morgan was fifteen, he received the ultimate healing from our Healing Rock (Jesus) when he was in a Jet Ski / boating accident, and he went to be with Jesus, our Healing Rock. His family misses him very much. His mother was so thankful he accepted Jesus as his Savior, so she knows he is in heaven with Jesus (our Rock) and with GG.

Magic
Healing
Rock

If you have never accepted Jesus as your Savior, please do so today. We don't know when we may die. We may be old, but we could be young. That is why we should always have our heart right with Jesus, because we never know when our time on earth is over. If you have never asked Jesus to forgive you of your sins (bad things we do), Romans 3:23 NKJV says, "For all have sinned and fall short of the glory of God." And you want to ask Jesus for forgiveness and make you His child, just say this prayer below with a sincere heart. 1 John 1:9 NKJV says, "If we confess our sins, He is faithful and just to forgive us our sins and to cleanse us from all unrighteousness."

Dear Jesus, I know I have sinned (disobeyed) you, and I'm sorry. Please forgive me and make me your child. Help me to live for you and each day grow to be more like you. Thank you for dying on the cross so I could have my sins forgiven and one day receive my ultimate healing from you the Healing Rock (Jesus). John 3:16 NIV says, "For God so loved the world that He gave His one and only Son, that whoever believes in Him shall not perish but have eternal life."

Morgan's mom lives for Jesus, and one day her desire is to receive the ultimate healing from Jesus, our Healing Rock, and see Jesus face-to-face and see Morgan and his GG again.

As Morgan says to his mom, "Let's stroll over heaven together as I show you all of the creation God has prepared for us."

About the Author

Elva Hainzey was born and raised in Revere, Pennsylvania. She moved to Ohio in 1965. She has been married to her husband, Chuck, for fifty-four years. They have five children and six grandchildren. She served in Children's Ministries for many years as a Sunday school teacher, director of a Mid-Week Bible Club, CLC (Christian Life Club), holding CLC in her neighborhood for many years, children's ministry and director for a few years, JBQ (Junior Bible Quiz) director for many years. Hainzey also worked with Kid's Camps for over twenty years and directed the camps for a few years. She is a member of Calvary Assembly of God in Willoughby Hills, Ohio.

CPSIA information can be obtained
at www.ICGtesting.com
Printed in the USA
LVHW070924130321
681412LV00001B/17

9 781636 308050